# MOUNTAINS

**Angela Wilkes**

**Illustrated by Peter Dennis**

**Revised by Felicity Brooks and Stephen Wright**

## Contents

Consultant: Edward Bates
Senior Lecturer
Whitelands College, Roehampton
Institute of Higher Education

# In the Mountains

High mountains are always cold, even in summer. And the higher you go, the colder it is. Often the snowy peaks are hidden by clouds.

A group or row of mountains is called a mountain range.

Eagle

It is too cold for trees to grow above a certain height on mountains. This height is called the tree-line.

Only evergreen trees grow high on mountains. They have tough, needle-like leaves which help them to stay alive through the winters.

Mountain goats

The top of a mountain is called the summit or peak.

The height above which there is snow all the year round on a mountain is called the snow-line.

A narrow gap between two mountains is called a pass.

Winds blowing from one direction have stunted and bent this tree.

Above the tree-line the ground is mostly rocky and bare. Some plants grow between the rocks, where they are sheltered from the cold winds.

Mountain flowers are small and have long roots to help them find water. They grow and flower in the spring and summer when it is warm.

3

# Living in the Mountains

People in the past often moved from the coasts and plains to escape invaders. They settled in the mountains. In Peru they built high fortress towns which they could defend from attack.

Mountain houses have thick walls to keep out the cold. In the Himalayas the animals live on the ground floor and the people live upstairs.

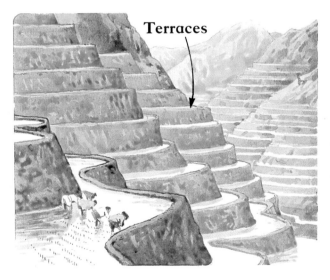

**Terraces**

It is hard to grow food on steep slopes. In the Philippines, farmers built terraces around the mountains and planted rice on the narrow steps.

Llamas

Mountain people are tough and can stand the cold. They carry huge loads on their backs.

They have few farm tools or machines. These women in the Himalayas are digging up potatoes.

People in Peru keep llamas. They carry heavy loads and their dung is used as fuel.

Women in the Andes weave their clothes from llama wool. They sell the brightly-colored cloth at village markets.

Monks have built many monasteries in mountains. They thought that the nearer they were to the sky, the nearer they were to their gods.

# Traveling in the Mountains

Yak

In the Himalayas there are few roads. Yaks carry loads along narrow tracks.

Strong porters carry baggage when the track is too steep and dangerous for yaks.

In some countries, where mountains are too steep to drive up, zig-zag roads have been built.

Crossing mountain rivers has always been difficult. Many are in deep gorges. In the Himalayas and Andes you can still see rope bridges.

These kind of bridges were first built hundreds of years ago. Crossing them is quite difficult because they sway easily.

Cable car

Cable cars carry people and supplies up mountains at ski resorts. Cabins on cables are wound up and down between the stations at each end.

Mountain railways need many tunnels and bridges. The Rhaetian railway in Switzerland has 376 bridges and 76 tunnels in 144 miles.

The Pilatus line in Switzerland is one of the world's steepest railways. The engine turns a toothed wheel in a toothed rail to drive it uphill.

# Wild Animals

These brown bears live in the forests on the lower slopes of the Rockies. They are big but are gentle unless hungry or scared.

Bears eat all kinds of food – berries, roots, insects and meat. They sharpen their long claws by scratching at the bark of trees.

Young bears are playful and can climb trees. They look for honey in wild bees' nests.

Brown bears are good at catching fish. They flip them out of the water with their paws.

Bears spend the winter asleep in dens. They dig deep holes in the ground or find dry caves.

# Hunters

**Timber wolf**

Timber wolves still roam mountain forests in North America. They hunt in packs, running very fast to catch and kill animals.

Pumas live in the Rockies and go hunting in the daytime. They creep up silently on very large animals, then leap on them and eat them.

## The hunted

**Snowshoe hare**

**Porcupine**

**Alpine marmot**

Snowshoe hares grow white coats in winter. This makes it hard for attackers to see them.

When the porcupine is in danger, its quills stand up and stick into anything they touch.

If danger is near, an Alpine marmot whistles to warn other marmots to dive into their burrows.

# In a Swiss Valley

In Switzerland, most mountain people live in the valleys, where there is good farmland.

This stream comes from melted snow high on the mountain.

Farmland

Hut where hay is kept

It is late summer in this valley in the Alps. The farmers are cutting the long grass and stacking it so that it will dry into hay.

When the winter comes, they will feed it to their cows, which are kept inside until the spring. Some cow's milk is made into butter and cheese.

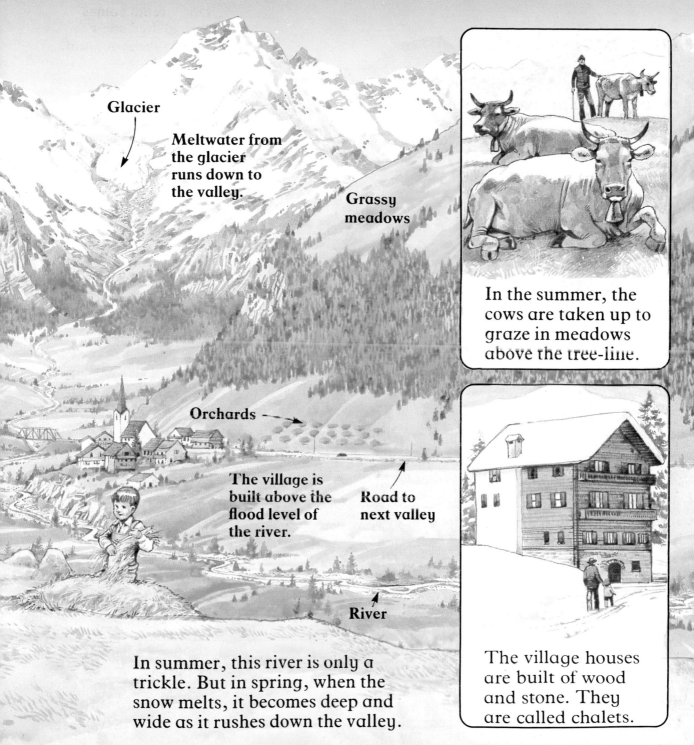

Glacier

Meltwater from the glacier runs down to the valley.

Grassy meadows

Orchards

The village is built above the flood level of the river.

Road to next valley

River

In the summer, the cows are taken up to graze in meadows above the tree-line.

The village houses are built of wood and stone. They are called chalets.

In summer, this river is only a trickle. But in spring, when the snow melts, it becomes deep and wide as it rushes down the valley.

# Above the Tree-line

High in the mountains there are bare, rocky slopes and cliffs.

It is too cold and windy for trees and most plants to grow there.

Eagle's nest

Golden eagle

These mountain goats live high in the Rockies, where they are safe from attackers. They have thick, shaggy coats to keep them warm.

They jump nimbly from ledge to ledge, looking for plants to eat. Special pads on their hoofs stop them from slipping on the rocks.

Golden eagle

The golden eagle glides high in the sky, searching for small animals. When it sees one, it swoops down and catches it in its claws.

The rare snow leopard lives in high, cold parts of the Himalayas. It sleeps in a rocky den during the day and hunts small animals at night.

Blue poppy

Mountain flowers grow under the snow. The edelweiss's fuzzy petals may help keep it warm.

Like most mountain flowers, the blue poppy flowers in the spring, when the snow melts.

This flower grows in cracks in the rock. It grows fluff around its petals to keep it warm.

# Above the Clouds

High mountain peaks are covered in ice and snow all the year round. Nothing can grow there. Under the ice and snow, there is only rock.

The peaks are sharp and jagged. Ice and frost split the rock so that bits of it break off and the shapes of the peaks slowly change.

**Griffon vulture**

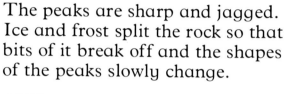

The wind is very strong at the top of a mountain. It blows the snow into strange shapes, or blows it away to show patches of bare rock.

One of the few signs of life high in the Himalayas are huge griffon vultures. They soar above the snow, looking for dead animals to eat.

The tops of mountains are often in sunshine above the clouds, but there is always the danger of bad weather and snowstorms.

Sometimes a mountaineer sees a strange shape, like a ghost, on the clouds below him. This is really a huge shadow of himself.

15

# Climbing the Peaks

Goggles

It is cold, high in the mountains. Climbers always wear warm clothes and thick boots.

They also wear goggles, because the sun and the glare from the snow could make them blind.

They clip spikes onto their boots. These help give them a firm foothold on slippery ice.

Ice axe

Oxygen mask

Climbers always rope themselves together. Each one also ties the rope to an ice axe which can be jammed into the snow if one of them slips.

There is very little air to breathe on high mountains. Climbers carry oxygen tanks on their backs and breathe the oxygen through masks.

# Winter Sports

Cable car

Skiers zig-zag down slopes so they do not go too fast.

Ski resort

This skier is jumping over a steep ridge.

Cross-country skiers

Ski school

In the winter, when the snow is deep, people go to the mountains for skiing vacations. Special resorts have been built for them.

People are taught to ski on gentle slopes. When they are good enough, they ski down steeper ones. Cable cars take them to the mountain tops.

17

# Avalanche!

An avalanche starts when a huge slab of snow begins to slide down a mountain. It may be set off by people walking on a slope.

An avalanche causes a huge rush of wind. The wind alone blew this bus off a mountain bridge. The snow itself did not reach the bridge.

Avalanches often start after a heavy snowfall, or in the spring when the snow begins to melt. This is an avalanche of powdery snow.

Moving faster and faster, it crashes downhill into the valley. It uproots trees and crushes or buries any houses in its way.

After an avalanche, rescue teams prod the snow to find people who have been buried in it.

Trained dogs sniff for people under the snow. If they are found quickly, they may still be alive.

Injured people are put on special stretchers. Helicopters carry them to the nearest hospital.

Roofs built over roads protect cars from the snow. An avalanche goes straight over the top.

Trees are planted on slopes above villages, to protect the villages from avalanches.

Soldiers fire at slopes to start small avalanches and stop the snow from building up.

# Conquering Everest

Everest is the highest mountain in the world. Many people had tried to climb it but had failed.

In March, 1953, John Hunt and twelve friends went to Nepal to try and reach the summit.

They set up camp at the base of the mountain. They practiced climbing for several weeks.

They hired local men to carry supplies. Their leader, Tenzing, was an experienced climber.

The climb was very dangerous. Sometimes they had to use ladders to cross crevasses.

The men climbed in groups, marking the way with flags in case snow later covered it.

There was a storm almost every day. It was very hard to walk because of strong winds.

The teams carried supplies up the mountain in relays. They set up camps along the way.

The night before they planned to climb to the top, there was a storm, which delayed them.

Tenzing and Hillary were chosen to climb the last peak. They ate a meal before starting.

They set off early in the morning. They were so high up, they had to wear oxygen masks.

When they reached the top, Hillary took photos to prove it. The date was May 23, 1953.

# Volcanoes

A volcano may look like any other mountain. People live and farm on the lower slopes.

There is a crater at the top of a volcano. It often puffs out smoke and ashes.

Where the Earth's crust is thin, hot liquid rock can break through to form a volcano.

Sometimes there is a huge explosion. Hot rocks, ash and gases shoot from the volcano.

Red-hot, liquid rock, called lava, pours out of the crater. It flows downhill, covering

anything in its way. As it cools, it hardens into rock and builds up the volcano.

This a cast of a body trapped in the ashes of Vesuvius which buried the town of Pompeii 79 AD.

Volcanoes sometimes erupt in the sea. In 1963 one erupted off the coast of Iceland and made a new island. It is called Surtsey.

Scientists sometimes go down inside volcanoes to find out more about them. They wear special suits to protect them from the heat.

# Mountains of the Moon

The Ruwenzori Mountains in Africa are called the Mountains of the Moon. They look mysterious and are often partly hidden in the clouds.

The peaks are always covered in snow, but it is hot all year round at the bottom. At different heights there are different plants and animals.

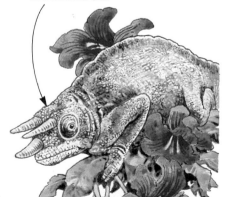

**Chameleon**

Above the grassy plains, there is jungle. Even though it is hot, it rains nearly every day.

This small chameleon lives in the jungle. Local people think that it brings bad luck.

Steamy bamboo forests grow at the next level. Bamboo sometimes grows over 3 feet a day here.

There is a cold, wet heath above the bamboo forest. Thick moss grows underfoot and the dripping trees are covered in lichen.

Strange plants and giant, spikey flowers grow among the beds of mosses. Small birds and some animals live even at this height.

Higher up there is bare rock. It is too cold for most plants to grow here. The lake is filled by water running down from a glacier.

The Mountains of the Moon have six peaks which are usually covered in clouds. It is very cold up here and snows nearly every day.

# Glaciers

**Hollow full of snow**

A glacier starts where snow heaps up on a slope high on a mountain. The snow packs together and turns to ice. The weight of any new snow then slowly pushes the ice downhill.

A glacier is a river of solid ice which creeps slowly down snow-covered mountains.

## Climbing a glacier

**The glacier only moves a few inches a day down the mountain.**

Climbers often use glaciers as a short cut up a mountain, but ice falls and huge blocks of ice can make them difficult to climb.

Glaciers have a lot of dangerous deep cracks in them. These are called crevasses. Some crevasses are as much as 100 feet deep. They are often hidden by snow.

## Crevasses

In winter, glaciers are covered in snow. The snow makes bridges across crevasses.

The bridges look safe but can be dangerous. They may collapse under a climber.

Climbers must be rescued from crevasses quickly, before they freeze to death.

The end of the glacier is called the snout.

This parking area is for tourists who have come to see the glacier.

These rocks and stones have been carried here by the glacier. They are called moraine.

Deep crevasses

A glacier carries along anything that falls on to it, such as rocks. A dead man once appeared at the end of a glacier. He had fallen into a crevasse almost 100 years before.

The glacier melts as it gets warmer lower down the mountain. Streams of meltwater from the end of the glacier run down to the valley.

# Mountains of the World

There are many shapes of mountains. These pointed peaks in France are called the 'needles'.

Some mountains have flat tops, like the Table Mountain in Cape Town, South Africa.

Other mountains have rounded tops. This mountain in Brazil is called the Sugar Loaf.

There are mountains all over the world. Some are in deserts. Some mountain ranges are under the sea and the tops are islands.

There are even mountains near the South Pole. They do not look high because the ice there is so deep that only the peaks show through.

A lot of wood comes from mountain forests. Lumberjacks chop down trees, then grow new ones. These logs are being floated to a sawmill.

Some of the world's most useful metals and precious stones are found deep inside mountains. Miners dig tunnels to find them.

Dam

In many valleys, rivers have been dammed to make lakes. The water is piped to towns, or used to drive machines which make electricity.

# Mountain Locations

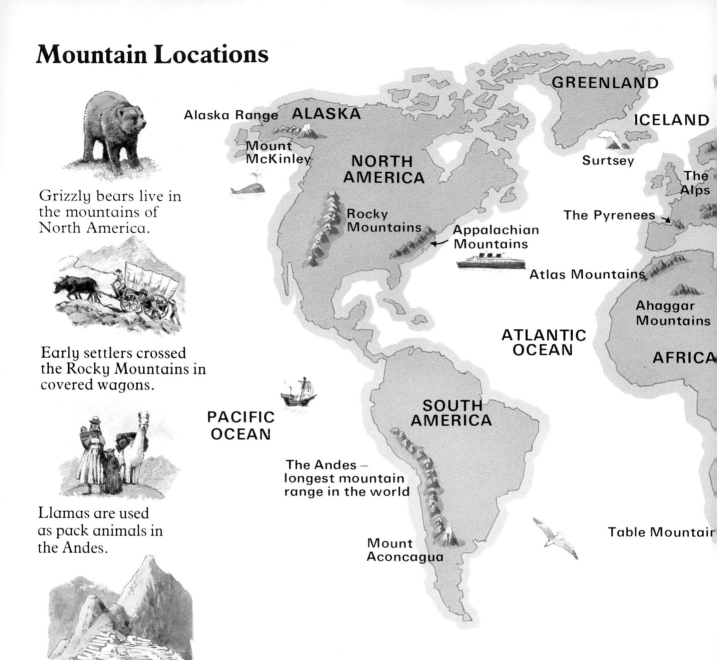

Grizzly bears live in the mountains of North America.

Early settlers crossed the Rocky Mountains in covered wagons.

Llamas are used as pack animals in the Andes.

Machu Picchu is a very old fortress town in the Andes.

Alaska Range ALASKA

GREENLAND

ICELAND

Mount McKinley

NORTH AMERICA

Surtsey

The Alps

Rocky Mountains

The Pyrenees

Appalachian Mountains

Atlas Mountains

Ahaggar Mountains

ATLANTIC OCEAN

AFRICA

PACIFIC OCEAN

SOUTH AMERICA

The Andes — longest mountain range in the world

Table Mountain

Mount Aconcagua

Scandinavia

Ural Mountains

ASIA

Former USSR

ROPE

Caucasus

Altai Mountains

CHINA

The Himalayas – world's highest mountain range

Fujiyama

JAPAN

Mount Everest

PACIFIC OCEAN

Ethiopian Highlands

Mountains of the Moon

Kilimanjaro

NEW GUINEA

INDIAN OCEAN

AUSTRALIA
Great Dividing Range

NEW ZEALAND

ANTARCTICA

Surtsey is an island made of volcanic lava.

Hillary and Tenzing were the first men to climb Everest.

The snow leopard lives in the Himalayas and Altai Mountains.

These grassy mountains are in China.

Many tribes live in the mountains of New Guinea.

# Index

Printed in Italy

# JUNGLES

**Angela Wilkes**

**Illustrated by Peter Dennis**

**Revised by Felicity Brooks and Stephen Wright**

## Contents

Consultants: Operation Drake

# In the Jungle

Jungles are thick, green forests that grow in hot, wet countries. They are also called rain forests because it rains nearly every day. Near the equator, where rain forests grow, there is no summer and winter. It is warm all year. Jungle trees grow very tall.

The trees and plants grow toward the light. They have flowers and fruit all year round.

There are many rivers in jungles because it rains so much.

Giant creepers with rope-like stems hang from the trees. They are called lianas.

The big trees shade the forest beneath from the sun. It can only shine through where there is a gap.

More than half of the world's animals and birds live in jungles. Most of them live in the trees.

# Walking through the Jungle

The jungle is gloomy at ground level, apart from patches of light. There is no wind and it is hot and steamy. The ground is covered in a thin layer of leaves and is often damp and squelchy. The tallest trees have wide roots, called buttress roots, which help to support them.

Where there is sun,
plants grow huge leaves.
Some have hooks which
catch on your clothes.

Many trees grow flowers
and fruit on their trunks,
like this South American
cannonball tree.

Old giant trees die and
crash to the ground.
Young trees spring up
in their places.

**Termite nest**

Termites look like
white ants. They eat
dead wood and build
their nests on trees.

Leaf-cutting ants take
bits of leaf back to
their nest. They grow
fungus on them to eat.

A lot of fungus grows
in the jungle. It helps to
rot down dead plants to
make new plant food.

# Where the Animals Live

When you are walking in the jungle, you cannot see the higher treetops, nor the animals that live in them.

Here you can see what size the different trees are, and find out which animals live there.

The tallest trees look like giant umbrellas. They shelter the jungle from the sun, rain and wind.

This level is called the canopy. Most of the flowers and fruit grow here.

The short trees grow so close together that very little sunlight can get through them.

It is quite dark at ground level. Only small plants grow here.

6

Large birds, such as monkey-eating eagles, fly at this height, looking out for prey.

Most birds live at this level. So do animals that climb and jump, such as monkeys. They eat fruit and leaves.

The trees are very thick here and hard to move through. Small animals and birds live in them.

Large animals that cannot climb trees, and many insects live on the rain forest floor.

To find out more about life in the treetops, scientists build observation platforms.

They also build high walkways, so that they can look at birds and flowers more closely.

# Moving through the Trees

Spider monkey

These South American spider monkeys use their tails to help them grip onto branches.

When a baby monkey cannot jump between branches, its mother makes a bridge for it.

The monkeys leap from one tree to another, looking for leaves and fruit they can eat.

Gibbon

Gibbons live in the Asian jungles. They are apes. These look like monkeys without tails.

Gibbons are great acrobats. They have very long arms and strong, hooked fingers.

They swing from hand to hand through the branches of trees at a tremendous speed.

**Tree frog**

**Flying lemur**

Some tree frogs look as if they can fly. Their webbed feet help them to glide when they jump.

The Asian flying lemur hangs upside down from the branch of a tree and sleeps during the day.

At night, it looks for food. Flaps of skin between its limbs help it to glide like a kite.

**Flying lizard**

**Flying snake**

Flying lizards also live in Asian jungles. When still, they look like ordinary lizards.

But when they jump, two flaps on their sides open out, and they can glide for a long way.

This Asian snake is called a flying snake. It can glide from one tree branch to another.

9

# The Rain Forest at Night

Howler monkey

Many jungle animals sleep all day and feed at night. As night falls, the jungle becomes very noisy. Howler monkeys start to call.

Frogs and toads gather in swamps and pools. They have very loud voices. They croak and squeak, hoping to attract a mate.

Pangolin

Mouse deer

Moon rat

Many small animals go to drink at water holes at night. They all have different ways of protecting themselves from enemies.

The pangolin is an anteater with horned scales that are like armor. The moon rat smells bad, and the tiny mouse deer can run very fast.

The fruit-eating bat has a face that looks like a fox.

Fruit-eating bats

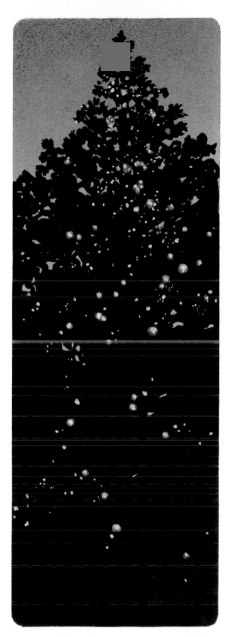

Fruit-eating bats hang upside-down in trees. They sleep during the day and feed at night.

They are the biggest bats in the world. They are also called flying foxes.

Loris

Some flowers bloom only at night. They are white and have a strong scent to attract moths.

Like many animals that come out at night, the loris has big eyes to help it see in the dark.

Male fireflies show off to female fireflies at night, by glowing with brilliant lights.

11

# The River Amazon

The Amazon is one of the biggest rivers in the world. It is really many rivers joined together.

Lots of birds and animals live along the banks of the rivers, or go there to drink and find food.

Hoatzin

Giant water lily leaves

Spoonbills wade in shallow water, looking for fish to catch.

Caiman

Baby hoatzin

The hoatzin is an odd bird. It can not fly very well but it can swim. The baby birds have claws on their wings to help them climb trees.

The caiman is a kind of alligator. It drifts along in the water, ready to snap at any fish or turtle it can eat.

12

Sandbank

Capybaras look like huge guinea pigs.

The anaconda is a giant snake. It squeezes small animals to death, then swallows them whole.

Scarlet ibis and egrets

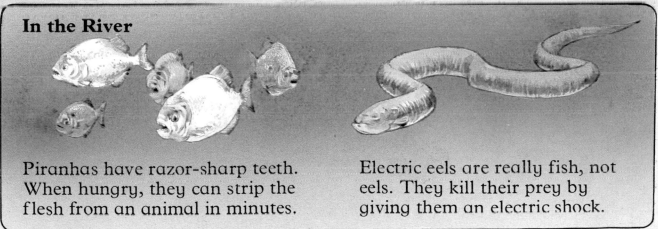

## In the River

Piranhas have razor-sharp teeth. When hungry, they can strip the flesh from an animal in minutes.

Electric eels are really fish, not eels. They kill their prey by giving them an electric shock.

# Why Rain Forests are Important

Rain forests are the home of many people and at least half the world's animals and plants. They also provide us with food, oxygen and materials for everyday things such as medicine, furniture and even chewing gum.

## Foods from the jungle

Cornflakes are made from corn.

All the world's chickens were bred from wild jungle fowl that live in the Indian rain forests.

Corn first grew in jungles in Central America. It is still an important food there.

Rice is the main food for over half the people in the world. It first grew in rain forests.

Peanuts, cashews and Brazil-nuts come from rain forest plants.

Chocolate is made from cocoa beans.

Coffee beans

Tea leaves → Cocoa pod

Tea, coffee and chocolate are made from the leaves or seeds of plants that first grew in the jungle.

Pineapples, oranges, bananas, lemons, eggplants and peppers come from jungle plants. Thousands of other jungle fruits and vegetables can be eaten.

Chewing gum is made from chicle. This comes from jungle trees.

Rain forest tribes know how to use many plants. The Lua tribe in Thailand grow over 120 plants for medicines, food, decoration and to make into clothes.

## Rubber

Collecting latex to make into rubber.

Rubber is made from a sticky liquid called latex. This is found in about 1,800 types of jungle plants and trees.

## Air

Jungles produce a lot of oxygen which goes into the air we breathe. When trees are cut down, there is less oxygen.

## Wood

Mahogany table

Balsa wood plane

Some of the most useful and beautiful kinds of wood such as balsa and mahogany come from rain forest trees.

## Medicines

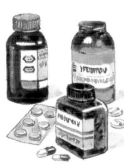

Chemicals from jungle plants are used in aspirin, antibiotics and quinine (used to treat malaria).

A quarter of all medicines are made from rain forest plants. Thousands of other plants can probably be used to make new medicines.

## Water

Clouds form from tiny drops of water joined together.

Water falls as rain from clouds.

A lot of water goes back into air from leaves.

River

Roots absorb water from ground.

Trees store water and release some of it back into the air. This helps to make more rain. If jungles are cut down, rain water runs away and it rains less. One billion people depend on rain water from jungles to grow their crops.

15

# Animal Disguises and Warnings

Small creatures stay alive by hiding from enemies. This tree snake is leaf-colored.

Some are camouflaged. This means they are hard to see against their homes, like this toad.

The chameleon changes the color of its skin as it moves among leaves and flowers.

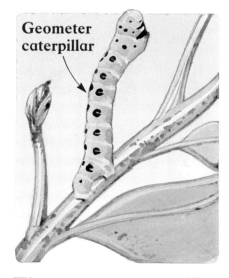

**Geometer caterpillar**

Some are disguised to look like something different. This leaf is really a butterfly.

This insect looks like a flower. It catches and eats insects which are searching for nectar.

The geometer caterpillar rears up and stays still, to look like a twig, when enemies are near.

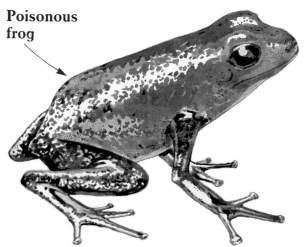

Poisonous frog

This Central American frog's bright colors warn its enemies that it is poisonous. Indians used to tip their arrows with its poison.

These poisonous butterflies also have warning colors. Harmless insects have copied the colors, so that enemies will avoid them too.

Coral snakes

These three coral snakes all look alike but one is poisonous. This confuses enemies and they do not know which snake to eat.

This is not an insect but a flower. It looks like a female bee and attracts male bees, who come and pollinate the flower.

# Strange Plants

Most plants need light to grow. As the jungle floor is dark, many plants grow high in the treetops, where there is more sunlight.

All the plants have ways of storing rainwater. This one traps it in cup-shaped leaves.

**Dead leaves rot down behind ferns to make soil for the plants.**

**Many plants have long roots which dangle in the air.**

The rafflesia grows in Asia. It is the world's biggest flower and smells of bad meat.

Most jungle orchids grow on trees. They store water in their leaves and stems.

A banyan starts when a seed grows on a branch of a tree. Its roots hang down the tree and strangle it. The banyan grow very wide as it spreads across the tree, putting down more roots.

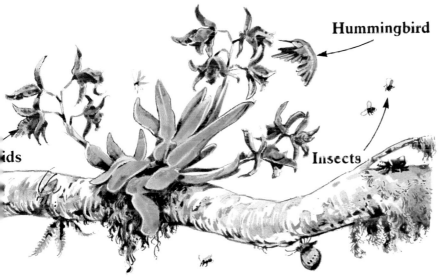

**Hummingbird**

ids

**Insects**

**Lianas**

Their bright color and scent attract insects, which come to feed on their nectar.

The insects carry pollen from one flower to another. This helps the orchids make new seeds.

Lianas twist themselves around trees and grow upward with them. They loop from tree to tree.

# Colorful Birds

Most jungle birds are brightly colored. This helps birds of the same kind to see each other.

The colors also help the birds hide among the bright leaves and flowers of the treetops.

Toucans

**Rainbow lorikeet**

This type of parrot lives in Australian jungles.

A toucan's beak may be as long as itself but is quite light. It uses it to reach for fruit.

It picks up berries with the tip of its beak and tips back its head to swallow them.

# Hummingbirds

Hummingbirds are tiny. One kind is no bigger than a bee. They live in the American jungles.

They beat their wings so fast that they make a humming noise. They hover when they feed.

Most hummingbirds have long beaks. They poke them into flowers to suck out the nectar.

# Birds of paradise

Birds of paradise were given their name because of their beauty. The males are brilliantly colored, but the females are plain and brown.

The males put on a show for the females, to help them choose their mates. They shriek, puff out their chests and show off their plumes.

# Living in the Rain Forest – 1

Parts of the world's rain forests are so hard to travel through that they have not been explored. But tribes have lived in the rain forests for thousands of years, seeing no one from the outside world. Their way of life has not harmed the rain forests.

The Pygmies live deep in the African rain forests. They do not grow crops to eat. Instead they collect wild plants and go hunting for animals.

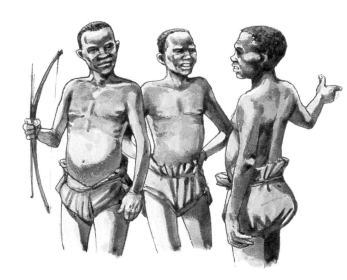

The Pygmies are small and can move quickly and quietly through the forest. They pick up any food they find and tuck it into their belts.

Pygmies live in small family tribes. They move from place to place, staying in each one for as long as they can find food there.

They set up their camps in clearings. The women make huts out of young trees and big leaves. Each hut has a fire in front of it.

The men hunt with bows and poison-tipped arrows. They also catch animals in huge nets.

The women cook vegetable stews. They add any meat that has been killed.

Afterwards the men sit around a fire, telling stories and singing songs about the forest.

# Living in the Rain Forest – 2

Some jungle tribes grow food as well as hunt. They cut down trees to make a clearing in the forest and then plant vegetables.

They build a village and fence in the crops to keep out animals. They stay in one village until no more crops will grow, then move on.

Some tribes in New Guinea keep wild pigs they have tamed, and treat them like pets.

In South America women grate, dry and sift roots to make flour for a type of bread.

Tribes who live near the Amazon fish as well as hunt. These men are making a dug-out canoe.

# Jungle homes

**This house is called a maloca.**

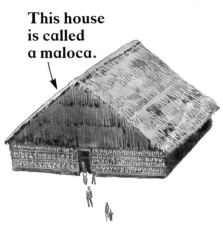

**This is called a stilt house.**

**This house is called a haus tambaran.**

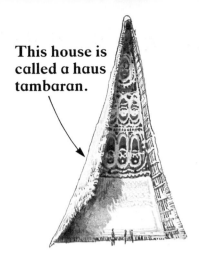

Some tribes build very unusual houses. A whole tribe lives in this South American maloca.

Some houses in South-East Asia are built on stilts, to help keep them dry and cool.

This is a special kind of religious house in Papua New Guinea. Only men are allowed in it.

## Changes

**Cocoa pods**

Life is changing for rain forest tribes. Many are now using money, and the children go to school.

Old tribal customs, such as war dances, are often only put on as shows for visiting tourists.

People now make money by growing crops to sell abroad, such as rubber and cocoa.

# Jungle Killers

Harpy eagle

Hunters rely on speed, strength and camouflage to catch their food. The harpy eagle glides silently among the tree-tops, looking for animals.

When it sees a group of small monkeys, the eagle swoops down very fast. It tries to seize one of them in its claws as the rest try to escape.

Big cats creep up quietly on their victims and attack them. Their spotted or striped coats are good camouflage in the rain forest.

Although it can run fast, a jaguar cannot chase its prey a long way. So it creeps as close as it can, then pounces and quickly kills it.

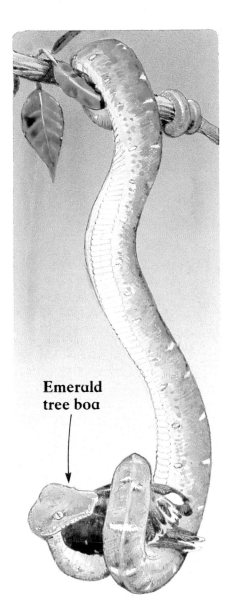

Pitcher plants trap insects which come to drink the sweet liquid around the plant's rim.

If an insect falls into the water in the plant and cannot climb out, the plant then eats it.

**Emerald tree boa**

This flower spider hides inside a flower and catches moths as they look for pollen.

The bird-eating spider hides on the ground. It can kill a small bird with one bite.

The color of the emerald tree boa acts as camouflage when it lies in wait for birds.

27

# The Death of the Rain Forests

All around the world, rain forests are being cut down. Every minute, about another 125 acres are destroyed or badly damaged. About half the world's rain forests and the animals that lived in them have already disappeared.

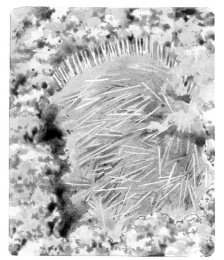

Many jungle tribes make clearings in the forest. They chop down trees and burn them.

Then they grow crops. But the soil is soon worn out and they have to make a new clearing.

Other people make money by chopping down trees for wood and using the land for beef cattle.

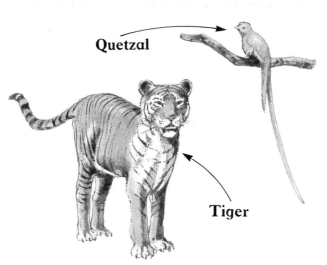

**Quetzal**

**Tiger**

Each animal has its own special place in the jungle. When trees are cut down, the animals and birds lose their homes and food.

If there are no other trees for them to move to, they cannot live. Many of them, like those above, are in danger of dying out.

Jungle tribes are being driven out of the jungle to live in towns. They are losing their homes, their land and their way of life.

When rain forests are chopped down, useless land is left behind. The soil is too poor to farm for long and the big trees cannot grow again.

# Jungle Locations

The jaguar is one of the biggest hunters in the Amazon jungle.

Hummingbirds live in jungles in Central and South America.

Many tribes of Indians live along the River Amazon.

Chimpanzees nest in the trees of the African jungle.

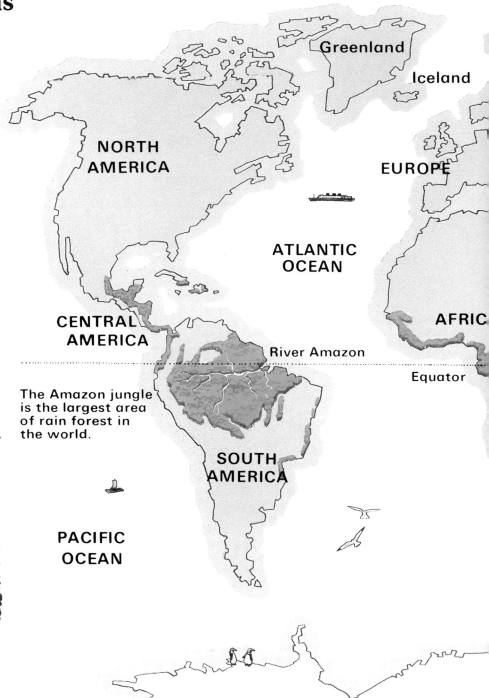

Greenland

Iceland

NORTH AMERICA

EUROPE

ATLANTIC OCEAN

AFRIC

CENTRAL AMERICA

River Amazon

Equator

The Amazon jungle is the largest area of rain forest in the world.

SOUTH AMERICA

PACIFIC OCEAN

30

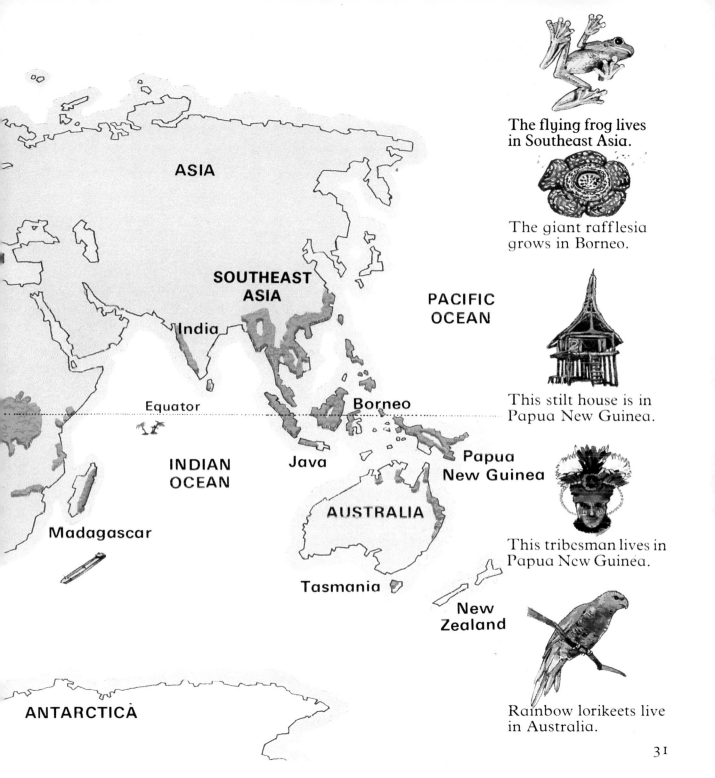

ASIA

SOUTHEAST
ASIA

India

PACIFIC
OCEAN

Equator

Borneo

INDIAN
OCEAN

Java

Papua
New Guinea

AUSTRALIA

Madagascar

Tasmania

New
Zealand

ANTARCTICA

The flying frog lives
in Southeast Asia.

The giant rafflesia
grows in Borneo.

This stilt house is in
Papua New Guinea.

This tribesman lives in
Papua New Guinea.

Rainbow lorikeets live
in Australia.

31

# Index

# DESERTS

**Angela Wilkes**

**Illustrated by Peter Dennis**

Revised by
**Felicity Brooks and Stephen Wright**

## Contents

Consultant: Dr. Andrew Warren
University College London

# In the Desert

Deserts are the driest places in the world. In parts of them, it may not rain for many years.

Most deserts are very hot in the daytime, but they cool off at night and can be very cold.

**When it rains, sand and stones are carried down from the hills by floodwater and left in fan-shaped patterns on the ground.**

Most deserts are rocky and bare. Parts of them are covered in sand. When the wind blows, the sand piles up into small hills called dunes.

Few plants and animals can live in the desert because it is too dry. The ones that are there all have ways of living without much water.

This plain floods after rain, but the rain soon dries up in the hot sun, leaving behind dry patches of salt.

Patch of salt

Caravan of camels taking salt across the desert

In parts of deserts, there are big, strange rocks. They may be all that is left of a mountain.

Where there is water, it may make an oasis – a place where trees and plants can grow.

Although it is hard to find water and food in the desert, some people live there. Many of them are nomads. They move around from place to place and set up their camps wherever they can find a well or a waterhole.

3

# How the Desert Changes

The wind does strange things in the desert. It whips up spiraling columns of dust.

The wind blows the sand so that it moves and changes direction like ripples on water.

If there is something in the sand's way, such as grass, the sand piles up behind it.

Dunes

The moving sand usually piles up to make a small dune. Sand blows up one side of a dune then slides down the other side, which is steeper.

The dune grows larger and moves forward very slowly. The sand around dunes is soft and vehicles can easily get stuck in it.

There was once a river in this desert. It made this channel thousands of years ago.

It washed broken rocks down from the hills. They now lie on the plains below.

Desert rocks slowly change all the time. Wind-blown sand wears them into odd shapes.

Sometimes just part of the rock wears away. This natural rock arch is in the state of Utah.

Many rocks are jagged. Sudden rain, heat or cold cracks them and then pieces break off.

These spiky rock towers in Bryce Canyon in Utah, were once part of an area of high, flat land.

# A Storm in the Arizona Desert

Big trees have very long roots to help them find water.

Saguaro cactus

This ocotillo bush has dropped its leaves so that it does not need so much water.

Sandy stream-bed

Many trees and bushes grow near dried-up streams, where water may be stored below the ground.

Prickly pear cactus

Everything that grows in the desert needs water. It has not rained here for many months and the ground is hard, dry and dusty.

The plants look dead, but they are alive. They all have ways of surviving in the dry season. Then when it rains, they grow and flower.

There are sometimes huge thunderstorms in parts of the desert. Then there is heavy rain. Water races down riverbeds and channels and floods across the plains. Even when the rain stops, the water may take weeks to sink into the ground or dry up in the sun.

**Spadefoot toad**

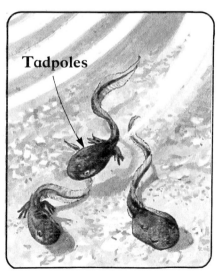

Tadpoles

After the rain, insects hatch and animals come out of their hiding places, like this toad.

It had buried itself to keep moist. Now it comes out to find a mate and lay eggs in the water.

The eggs hatch into tadpoles, which grow into toads before the pools of water dry up.

# After the Rain

After the rain, green shoots push their way up out of the damp ground, and parts of the desert may be covered in a carpet of flowers.

They have grown from seeds that may have been lying there for many years. The seeds will not grow unless there is plenty of rain.

The flowers only bloom and live for a few weeks, while there is still enough water for them.

Insects come to drink nectar from them and spread pollen from one flower to another.

The flowers then make new seeds which drop to the ground and flower after the next rain.

Some plants can live in the desert all the year round because they store water.

Prickly pear cactus

Barrel cactus before rain

Barrel cactus after rain

Spines

There are many kinds of cactus in America. They have tough skins but are juicy inside.

When it rains, their widespread roots soak up water and their stems swell to store it.

Cacti have flowers, but have spines, instead of leaves, to protect them from thirsty animals.

Saguaros

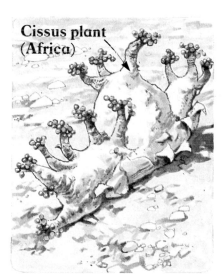

Cissus plant (Africa)

Welwitschia plant (Africa)

They grow very slowly, but some grow very tall. Cacti like this may be over 100 years old.

This shrub also stores water in its stem. Some desert trees store water in their trunks.

This plant collects dew on its leaves. Drops of water then drip to the ground above its roots.

# Birds that live in the Desert

Desert birds all have special ways of living with the heat and shortage of water.

Ostrich

The ostrich can go for days without drinking. It breathes fast to help it keep cool.

Flocks of budgerigars live in the Australian Outback. They drink at waterholes.

If it does not rain for a long time and the waterholes dry up, thousands of them die.

Sand grouse

Birds that eat seeds must drink every day. The sand grouse flies a long way to find water.

It wets its breast feathers and flies back to its chicks, who suck the water from them.

Vultures

Vultures keep cool by soaring high in the sky. Their sharp eyes can spot a dead animal to eat from many miles away. When they see one, they swoop down to feed. They get the liquid they need from their prey's blood. Small birds get liquid by eating juicy insects.

Birds must shield their eggs from the sun. The gila woodpecker builds its nest in a cactus.

When it leaves the hole it has made, another bird, such as this owl, moves in.

The burrowing owl makes its nest in a burrow that a prairie dog once lived in.

# Surviving in the Desert

Deserts are so hot in the daytime that most animals would die if they stayed in the sun for long.

Most desert animals, like these American ones, seek shelter from the sun during the hottest part of the day.

Saguaro cactus

A bobcat dozes in the shade of a bush or rock, panting to help it keep cool. It goes hunting at night, when the desert is cooler.

The American desert tortoise sometimes burrows underground to hide from the sun.

Horned lizard partly buried in the sand.

Coral snake

Reptiles, such as snakes and lizards, have tough leathery skins to protect them, but even they look for shade when it is hot.

Desert animals must be able to live without much water. Most of them get the liquid they need from the plants or insects they eat.

Jack rabbit

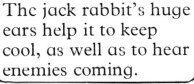

The jack rabbit's huge ears help it to keep cool, as well as to hear enemies coming.

Addax antelope

The addax antelope lives in the Sahara. It does not drink any water at all.

Camels can go without water for weeks, but then they drink gallons at a time.

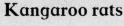

Sidewinder rattlesnake

This rattlesnake has buried itself in the sand to keep cool, and to lie in wait for victims.

**Kangaroo rats**

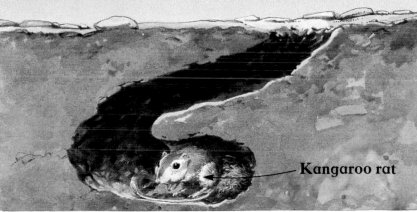

Kangaroo rat

The kangaroo rat digs a shallow burrow where it can hide and sleep during the day.

It does not drink any water. It gets all the moisture it needs from the seeds it eats.

# Hunters and the Hunted

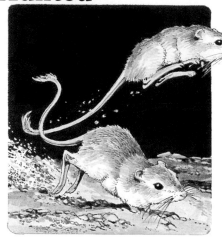

Most desert animals hunt at night. The kit fox's sand-colored fur is good camouflage.

It hunts kangaroo rats. They jump high, kicking sand in the fox's face, then run away.

Some lizards, like this Australian one, have a spiny skin to protect them from enemies.

## How a rattlesnake hunts

Kangaroo rat

The rattlesnake is poisonous, but it will not attack large animals unless it is frightened. It shakes the rattle on its tail as a warning.

At night, when it is hunting, the snake is quiet. Small pits near its eyes and its forked tongue help it to sense when a small animal is near.

14

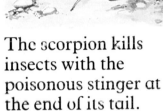

When this Australian lizard is in danger, it puffs out its frill to frighten its attacker.

The scorpion kills insects with the poisonous stinger at the end of its tail.

The trapdoor spider makes traps for insects. When insects fall in, the spider eats them.

The snake glides silently forward, then it quickly strikes. It sinks its poisonous fangs into its prey and then it lets go.

The animal runs away but dies very quickly. The snake goes after it. When it finds the dead animal, it swallows it whole.

# Living in the Desert – 1

Living in the desert is difficult because water and food are hard to find. Many desert people are nomads and move from place to place.

The Tuaregs are nomads who live in the Sahara. They are herdsmen and travel from well to well, looking for pastures for their animals.

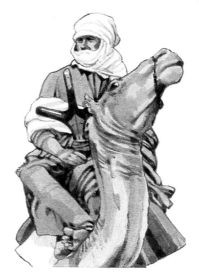

The Tuaregs were once fierce warriors who led great camel raids. They do not fight now.

They wear loose robes, to keep cool. They hang charms around their necks to ward off evil.

Tuareg men keep their faces veiled. The veil, called a tagilmust, is almost 20 feet long.

The Tuaregs keep camels, goats and sheep. They always camp near a well or waterhole, where the animals can drink and graze.

The women or children fetch water for the camp. They carry it in goatskin containers, which they sling under their mules.

Belongings in tree, out of reach of animals

Animals

Water container hanging from trestle

Tuaregs live in tents, which they carry with them. The tents are usually made of goatskins stitched together and stretched over poles.

The women collect firewood and cook the food. Here one woman is making bread while the other grinds corn to make a kind of flour.

17

# Living in the Desert – 2

Not all nomads are like the Tuaregs. The San people of the Kalahari Desert do not keep herds, but collect plants to eat and hunt animals.

They wander from place to place, making grass huts to sleep in at night. Their way of life has not changed for thousands of years.

Every day the women look for roots to eat. They can spot plants even in the driest ground, and then dig them up with sharp sticks.

The men go hunting, using spears and poisoned arrows. There are few animals in the Kalahari and the hunters must track them down.

The San know how to find water under the ground. They suck it up through hollow reeds.

Empty ostrich egg

Sometimes they store water in buried ostrich egg shells, so that they can drink it later.

Australian Aborigines used to live like the San people, but now most of them live in towns.

When there is a long drought, the waterholes dry up and some nomads move to towns.

Many nomads are now learning to read and write, so they can get jobs if they desire.

More and more men who were nomads get jobs on farms or work in mines to earn a living.

19

# A Sahara Salt Caravan

Some goods are still taken across the desert by caravans of camels. This Tuareg is packing salt to take across the Sahara and sell.

Camels are loaded with the heavy bundles. They can travel for several days without any water but they are sometimes bad-tempered.

The camels are tied together so they follow the leader and cannot run away. The men ride them when the sand is too hot to walk on.

The Tuaregs do not use maps to cross the desert. Instead they use the sun and stars as well as familiar landmarks to guide them.

Camels are hard to learn to ride.
They sway back and forth and from
side to side. Tuaregs steer them with
their feet and a rope.

Camels must drink every few days
when they are carrying heavy loads.
Tuaregs can sometimes find water
under the sand between the wells.

When there is a sandstorm, it is
impossible to travel. The caravan has
to stop and the men seek shelter from
the sand until the storm is over.

The caravan stops at night and the
men sit around a fire drinking tea
and telling stories. They sleep
wrapped in blankets on the ground.

21

# Oases

An oasis is a place in the desert where there is water. The water comes from a spring or river. In an oasis trees and plants can grow.

Most oases, like this one in Tunisia, have towns built around them. People can live here because there is always a supply of water.

People grow fruit trees and vegetables. Date palms grow easily and are useful for food and wood. This man is cutting dates.

There are two kinds of markets in Tunisian oasis towns. This is a food market. The food is piled up on woven mats on the ground.

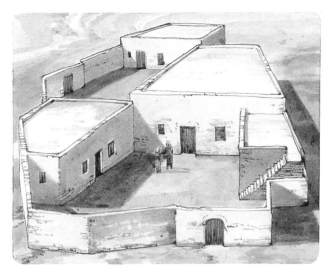

A covered market is called a souk. Here most things are sold apart from food. Caravans bring goods from across the desert to these markets.

Houses in an oasis are usually made of mud or plaster. Their thick walls, flat roofs and small windows help to keep them cool inside.

## Underground homes

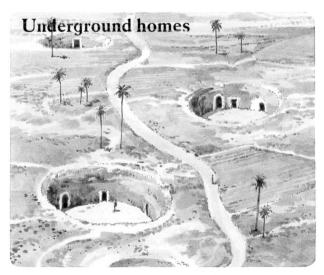

## Homes in the rocks

Some desert people live in very strange places. The Matmatans of Tunisia build their houses under the ground, where it is cooler.

On the edge of the desert, in Turkey, people build houses in these rocks. They hollow out the insides and put in windows and doors.

# Strange Sights in the Desert

Mirage

Thirsty travelers crossing deserts sometimes think they can see a lake in front of them. But as they move closer, the water disappears.

It is a trick of the light called a mirage. Hot air above the ground acts like a mirror. It reflects the sky and looks like water on the ground.

This is also a mirage. These camels are on dry land, but they look as if they are walking in water and we can see their reflections.

Sometimes dark clouds form and it looks as if it is starting to rain, but the hot air dries up the rain before it reaches the ground.

# The Desert's past

In some deserts, there are strange tree trunks made of stone. They are fossils of trees that grew in forests there 100 million years ago.

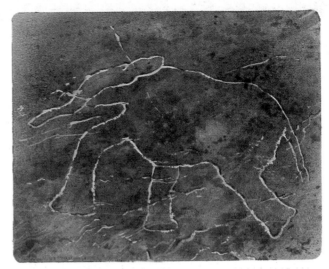

Deserts were not always as dry as they are now. Cave paintings in the Sahara show that animals, such as elephants, once roamed there.

In some places, there are ruins of old cities. There was once an oasis here, but the water dried up and the people had to move away.

This plain was once a lake. As the water began to dry up, it got saltier. Then it dried up completely and left a desert covered with salt.

# Things that come from the Desert

Deserts are important for many reasons. They are the homes of people and animals, but they also provide materials such as diamonds and oil.

**Oil well in the Arabian Desert**

Oil and natural gas have been found under the Arabian, Sahara, American and Australian deserts. Scientists are always searching for more.

In Australia, uranium, nickel and alumina (to make into aluminum) are mined. Australia mines more alumina than any other country.

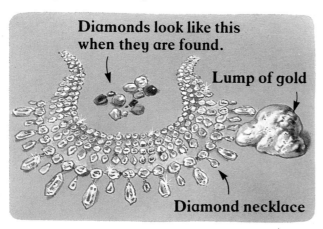

**Diamonds look like this when they are found.**

**Lump of gold**

**Diamond necklace**

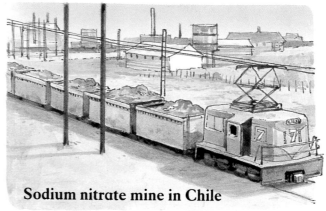

**Sodium nitrate mine in Chile**

Gold and diamonds have been found under the deserts in Australia, Namibia and South Africa. South Africa produces the most.

The Atacama Desert in Chile is the driest in the world, but has a lot of sodium nitrate. This is used to make fertilizers which help plants grow.

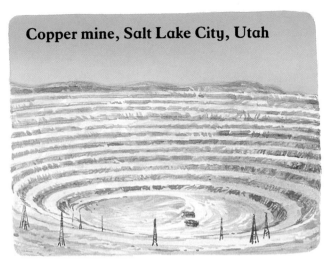

Copper mine, Salt Lake City, Utah

Chile also produces more copper than any other country. There are copper mines in the deserts of Australia, America and Mexico, too.

Many desert people now travel by car but still keep camels.

These discoveries mean that some desert countries have become richer. They have built roads, railways, airports and towns in the desert.

Power from the sun

Solar-powered car

Solar-powered telephone

Scientists have found ways of changing the sun's heat into power to run things. This is called solar power. It is very useful in deserts.

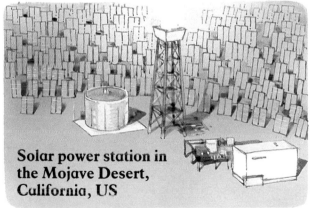

Solar power station in the Mojave Desert, California, US

The biggest solar power station is in the Mojave Desert where there are more than 300 sunny days each year. It cost 142 million dollars to build.

27

# Making things grow in the Desert

Parts of some deserts are becoming even barer. People chop down trees for firewood, and their animals eat all the plants.

In some places, steady winds blow from one direction. If the wind brings sand toward an oasis, dunes build up, burying houses and trees.

Now people are trying to grow crops in the desert. In Iran, they spray oil on to sand dunes. This dries to a kind of thick crust.

Trees are planted in it and are protected from animals. When they grow, they help to keep the sand in place and make the soil richer.

Rivers flowing through desserts are dammed. Water can thenbe chaneled to nearby land and used to grow fruit and vegetables.

In Israel, plants are grown in plastic tents. When the plants are watered, the plastic stops the water from drying up in the hot sun.

The Imperial Valley in California used to be part of a big desert. Now fruit and vegetables are grown there all the year round.

To make the valley green, a canal was built to bring water from the Colorado river, almost 80 miles away. It is piped to all the fields.

# Desert Locations

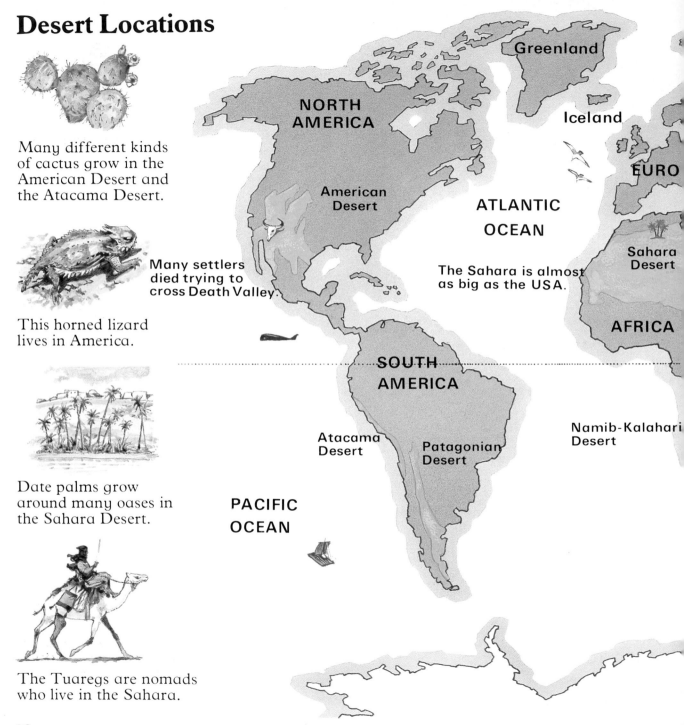

Many different kinds of cactus grow in the American Desert and the Atacama Desert.

This horned lizard lives in America.

Date palms grow around many oases in the Sahara Desert.

The Tuaregs are nomads who live in the Sahara.

Greenland

Iceland

NORTH AMERICA

American Desert

ATLANTIC OCEAN

EURO

Sahara Desert

AFRICA

SOUTH AMERICA

Atacama Desert

Patagonian Desert

Namib-Kalahari Desert

PACIFIC OCEAN

Many settlers died trying to cross Death Valley.

The Sahara is almost as big as the USA.

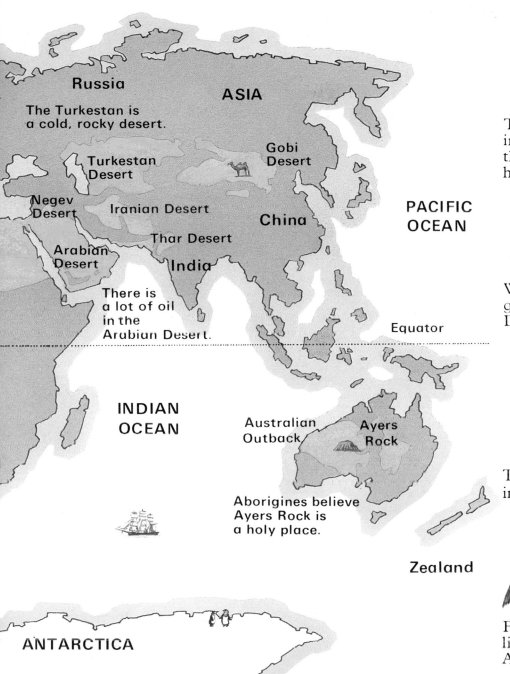

Russia

ASIA

The Turkestan is
a cold, rocky desert.

Gobi
Desert

Turkestan
Desert

Negev
Desert

Iranian Desert

China

PACIFIC
OCEAN

Thar Desert

Arabian
Desert

India

There is
a lot of oil
in the
Arabian Desert.

Equator

INDIAN
OCEAN

Australian
Outback

Ayers
Rock

Aborigines believe
Ayers Rock is
a holy place.

Zealand

ANTARCTICA

The camels that live
in cold deserts, like
the Gobi, have two
humps and thick fur.

Welwitschia plants
grow in the Namib
Desert.

The San people live
in the Kalahari Desert.

Flocks of budgerigars
live in the dry
Australian Outback.

# Index

Printed in Italy